For my darling Sadie, my pal Chase, and my adorable Rose—B. M.

For my buddy, Jackson—B. D.

Text © 2009 Creative Concepts LC
Illustrations © 2009 Brandon Dorman

Visit us at ShadowMountain.com

Library of Congress Cataloging-in-Publication Data

Mull, Brandon, 1974–
 Pingo / Brandon Mull.
    p. cm.
  Audience: K–3.
  Summary: Teased by his friends for having an imaginary playmate, Chad tries to bid Pingo farewell but Pingo refuses to leave.
  ISBN 978-1-60641-109-4 (hardbound : alk. paper)
 [1. Imaginary playmates—Fiction. 2. Friendship—Fiction.] I. Title.
 PZ7.M9112Pin 2009
 [E]—dc22
                                                           2009003268

Printed in Mexico
RR Donnelley, Reynosa

10   9   8   7   6   5   4   3   2   1

PINGO

Written by **Brandon Mull**

Illustrated by **Brandon Dorman**

SHADOW
MOUNTAIN

Like many other kids his age, Chad
had an imaginary friend. That friend
was named Pingo.

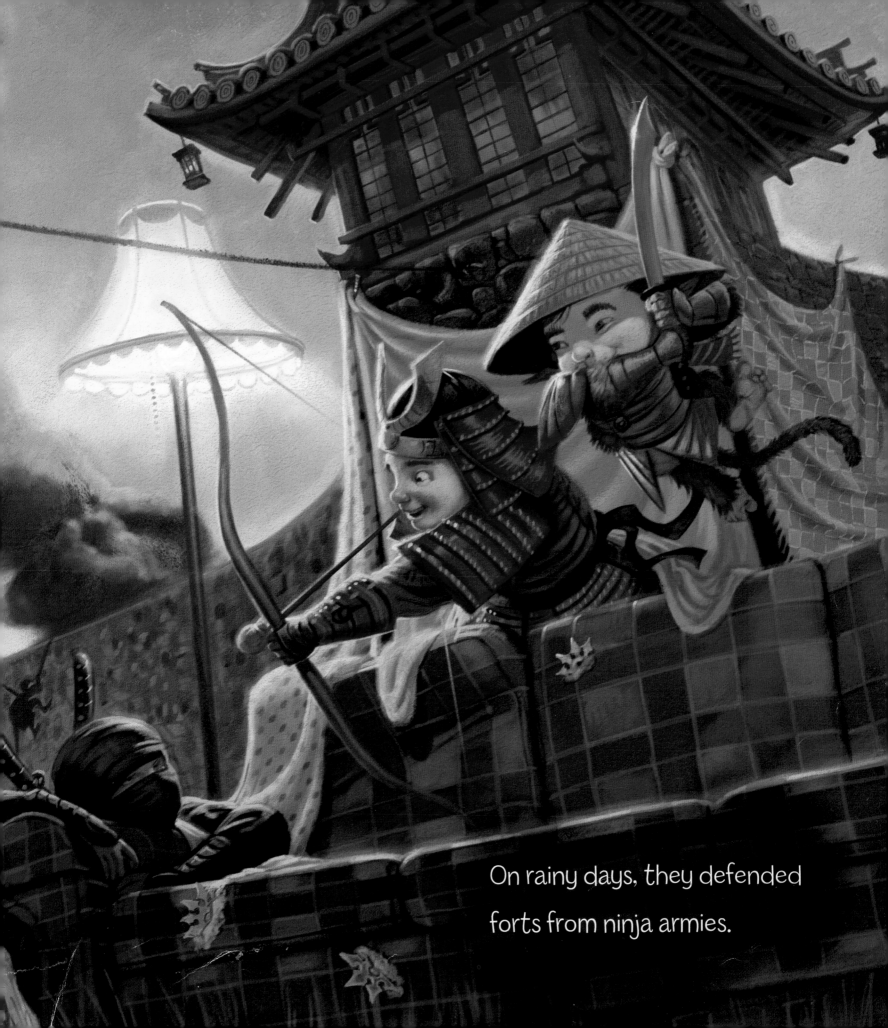

On rainy days, they defended forts from ninja armies.

Sometimes they brewed magical potions.

And sometimes Chad's room became a zero gravity chamber.

As Chad grew older, he was often taunted for having an imaginary friend.

One day, Chad got fed up with the teasing and sat down with Pingo to have a talk.

"I'm growing up," Chad said. "It's time to stop pretending that you're real."

"Pretending?" Pingo asked.

"That's right," Chad said. "If I stop believing in you, you'll disappear!"

"I'm not so sure about that," Pingo said.

"Wanna bet?" Chad said. "We've had some fun, but I'm done playing. Good-bye, Pingo."

"But wait," Pingo said. "I'm still here! We'll see whether the playing is done . . ."

From that day forward, Chad no longer had an imaginary friend.

He had an imaginary enemy!

Pingo led pirate raids when Chad was trying to sleep.

Pingo filled Chad's backpack with maple syrup and peanut butter.

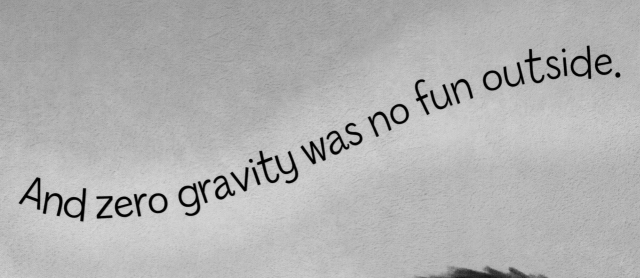

And zero gravity was no fun outside.

Eventually Pingo grew weary of harassing Chad. As the years passed, Pingo bothered him less and less.

Occasionally a report that Chad
needed for work would vanish.

By the time Chad was an old man living in a quiet rest home, he had almost forgotten about his old friend who was also his old enemy.

Until one day Chad could not find his dentures. He checked under the bed, in his dresser drawers, and in the bathroom sink.

When he looked in the closet, he found Pingo showing off a new set of perfect teeth. Chad couldn't help but laugh.

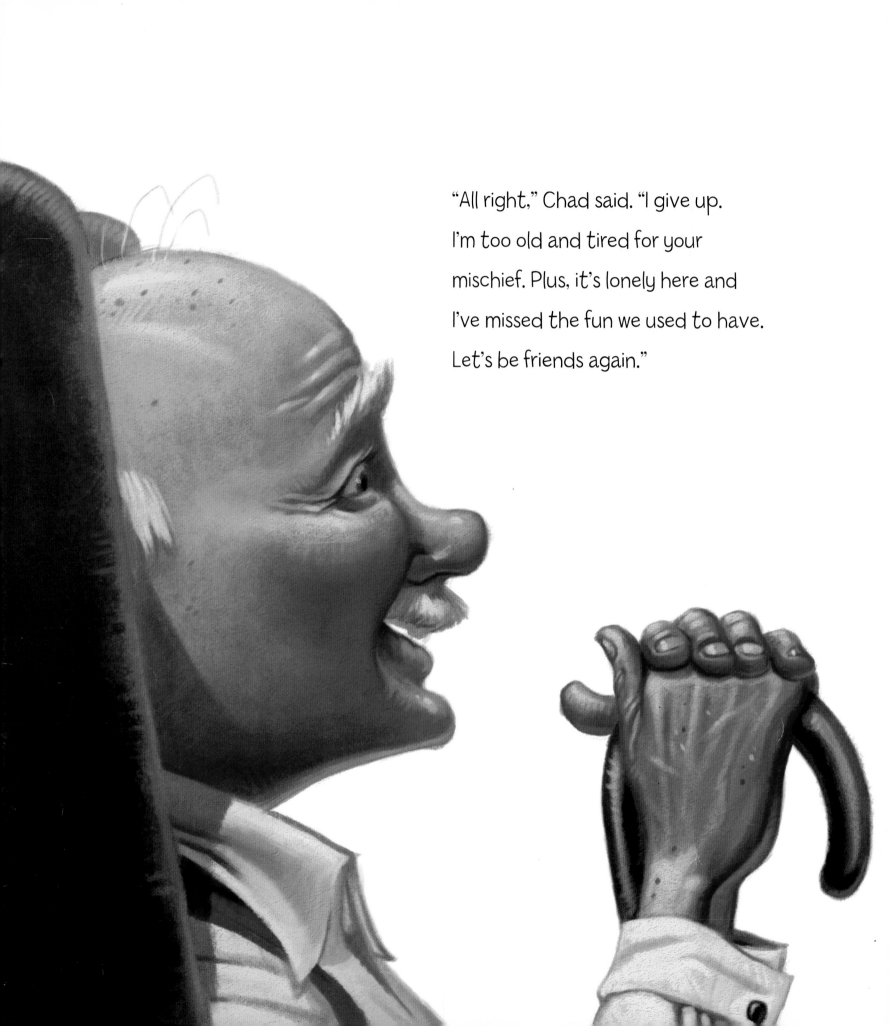

"All right," Chad said. "I give up.
I'm too old and tired for your
mischief. Plus, it's lonely here and
I've missed the fun we used to have.
Let's be friends again."

"That's all I ever wanted to hear,"

Pingo said with a smile.

Before Chad knew it he and Pingo were on safari in Africa.

Escaping spies on jet skis.

And counseling with the wise chiefs of mighty tribes.

Chad and Pingo lived
happily ever after.